The Monster at Recess

The Monster at Recess

SHIRA POTTER

HEART LAB

Heartlab Press Inc.
www.heartlabpress.com

Ordering Information:
Quantity sales. Special discounts are available on quantity purchases by corporations, associations, and others. For details, contact the publisher at the address above.
Orders by U.S. trade bookstores and wholesalers.
Printed in the United States of America Second Edition: Revised 2017 Edition
ISBN: 978-0-9950441-6-6

Chapter 1

Sophie froze in her seat. A few of the other students laughed. She knew she should know the answer to the question, but she didn't. Somewhere the answer was in her mind. Yet, she couldn't get that answer out into words.

"Sophie," Mrs. Cook said. "Have you been listening at all today?"

Sophie nodded.

Mrs. Cook turned her attention to Julia who had her hand raised high in the air. "Julia."

"To make 'news' a compound word, you can add the word, 'paper.'"

"Very good Julia." Mrs. Cook smiled.

Sophie looked out the window at the

playground. The monsters at Monstmasta Day School played about. They had recess before her school. Both schools used the same playground. The girls at her school, Grey Stone Day School, were not supposed to talk to the monsters. This is why they had recess at different times. To keep them apart.

"Sophie, pay attention," Mrs. Cook said. "There will be a quiz and I expect you to get it right."

Sophie turned her face forward. Mrs. Cook continued her lesson. Sophie glanced out the window with only her eyes. She made sure not to turn her head, in order not to draw the attention of Mrs. Cook.

She watched the monsters as they played tag. She liked watching them. All the monsters were different colors; pinks, reds, blues and greens. She looked around the classroom at her fellow students dressed in black and gray. The monsters definitely looked like they were having more fun.

As Sophie was walking home from school, she heard some girls giggling. She glanced behind her. Julia and Molly both smiled. Molly whispered something to Julia. Sophie heard the word, "weirdo." Again, Sophie froze. Her stomach knotted. The girls rushed past her, knocking into her. Sophie dropped a gray glove. She bent down to pick it up and she couldn't believe her eyes. On the ground, in the same spot was a multi-colored hat. It must have been dropped by one of the monsters. Sophie picked it up and examined it. This had to be the most colorful thing that she had ever seen up close. She quickly stuck it in her pocket.

Chapter 2

At recess, Sophie tried on the multicolored hat in front of the bathroom mirror. It was a bit small but the red brought out her green eyes. She heard laughter and the bathroom door burst open. Sophie quickly ripped the multicolored hat off her head and hid it in her pocket.

Girls from her class ran in. They fixed their hair in the mirror. One girl put on lip gloss. They completely ignored her existence. She hadn't needed to hide the hat after all. Unlike Julia and Molly, these girls weren't mean to her. However, instead of insulting her, they made her feel completely invisible. She wasn't sure if she preferred the outright meanness of Julia and Molly or these girls who didn't even acknowledge that she was in the room. To them, she was invisible.

She didn't know why they chose not to include her in their groups. At the kindergarten, she had gone to, she had been well liked. But, at this school, it appeared that everyone hated her and she couldn't figure out why. When she had gone to an interview before being accepted into Grey Stone Day School, Principal Lovell had looked at her.

"She'll have to do something about her hair," the principal had said.

"Excuse me?" Sophie's mom had responded.

"Her hair, she colors it. She'll have to stop."

Sophie's Mom had laughed. "Colors it? She's a natural red-head."

"I see," Principal Lovell had said.

In class, Sophie looked around at the other students. Their hair was all brown. They wore it in ponytails, and so did she.

Her hair was also now brown. She had begged her mom to color it, to be like the other girls. She thought this way, they'd accept her. But. It. Didn't. Make. A. Difference.

She looked at the multi-colored hat in her pocket. The hat made her happy but she knew it was wrong of her to keep it. It wasn't hers. She had to return it somehow. But how? Everyone in her school spoke about how the monsters were bad. How they steal and spit on you when you're not looking. She had once seen Molly out the window, spitting a giant glob of spit, down into the monsters playground. It had hit a small monster. Molly and Julia had both laughed. Then, another time, Molly had found a locket on the ground. It belonged to one of the monsters as it had a picture of one of them in it. They could have left it there but Molly walked off with it. Sophie felt the hat in her pocket. She needed to return it. She didn't want to be like them.

"Sophie," Mrs. Cook yelled, "Sophie." Sophie looked up. She had been so lost in thought that she had forgotten where she was. She was in class. The other students laughed.

"Sophie, do you think you can do that?" Mrs. Cook asked.

"Do what?" Sophie asked.

The other students laughed some more.

"Go to the library and pick up the books," Mrs. Cook said, sternly.

Sophie nodded. On her way to the library, she had a thought. *The monsters are having their recess now.* She was only a few steps from the library. She knew she should follow Mrs. Cook's instructions. Yet, instead she turned to face the school door. She ran to it and threw it open. Daylight shone brightly. The monsters were on the playground, running about. She stepped outside into the warm sunlight.

Chapter 3

Sophie watched all the monsters running about, and felt a twinge of doubt. She wasn't one of them. They'd know for sure. What if they harmed her? The hat, she remembered. She could use the hat as a disguise. She reached into her pocket and placed it on her head. It fit. She pulled it down so she'd be even less noticeable.

"Hey," a voice yelled at her. Sophie froze. She breathed in and out. "Tag, you're it," the voice said.

Sophie turned around. She saw a female monster standing there. She was purplish pink, with red stars all over face. Her hair was a mess of blue ringlets. The monster ran into the middle of the playground.

Sophie felt relieved. They didn't recognize her. She was safe. She smiled to herself. Then, she ran into the playground. All around her were different colored monsters. She ran up to a green monster and touched him on his slimy shoulder.

"Tag, you're it!" Sophie yelled in delight, squishing the gooey slime in her hand. The green monster chased her. She laughed and ran away.

Sophie ran into the outdoor stairway of the monster's school. The green monster cornered her.

"You don't look like us," he said.

Sophie froze. Maybe her plan was silly after all. How could a hat disguise her?

The purplish pink monster appeared. "What are you talking about, Beaty? Of course she does. Look at her hat."

The female monster pulled Sophie to the slide. Together they had so much fun sliding down again and again.

"What's your name?" the female monster asked.

"Sophie," Sophie said.

"Sophie? What a strange name," the monster said.

"What's your name?" Sophie asked.

"Zaragilda," the monster replied.

"Strange," Sophie said.

"No it's not," the monster said. "I know ten girls who are called that here. I'd love to have your name."

"Why? Isn't it better to be like everyone else?" Sophie asked.

"Are you kidding?" Zaragilda said. "It's so much more fun to be different."

Recess ended and Sophie returned to class. She was about to enter the classroom when she remembered the books. She spun around and rushed to the library and picked up the box. The box that she was instructed to deliver over ten minutes ago.

"Well you took a long time," Mrs. Cook scolded.

"Ssssorry," Sophie said. "They couldn't find them."

Mrs. Cook went back to teaching. Sophie smiled to herself. She put her hand inside her pocket and felt the hat. She would return it tomorrow.

Chapter 4

The next day at school, Sophie waited eagerly for Mrs. Cook to ask her to do something, but Mrs. Cook didn't. Sophie raised her hand to go to the bathroom. Mrs. Cook nodded. Sophie only had a few minutes but it would still be better than nothing. Today she would return the hat as she had intended to do so the day before.

She went outside into the playground. All the monsters ran about. Where was Zaragilda? She couldn't find her. Sophie was about to give up when she saw Zaragilda by the climbing wall. She ran up to her.

"Come join me," Zaragilda said.

Sophie looked towards the school. Mrs.

Cook would notice she was missing. Or ... maybe she wouldn't. Sophie joined Zaragilda climbing up the tower. Together, they reached the top.

"I've never gotten this far before," Zaragilda gushed.

Together, they looked down at everyone. Then, Sophie looked across. She could see the other students in her classroom. A thought occurred to her that someone could look out. Someone could see her. And then what? She'd be even more hated than she currently was. They'd make fun of her even more. They'd call her, "Monster Girl."

Sophie quickly climbed down from the tower and ran back to the classroom. She was sure someone had seen her, but when she entered the classroom, everything was normal. Even Mrs. Cook was where she was when Sophie had left her. At her desk, marking papers.

After class as Sophie headed home, she felt the hat inside her pocket. She still knew she should return it. But now, she didn't want to. She wanted to keep hanging out with Zaragilda. The only way to do so, would be to keep the hat. *No,* she thought to herself, *I won't return it.*

Chapter 5

The next day at school, Sophie was finally able to get out of class. Mrs. Cook asked her to get the orange juice. However, this time, she was sent downstairs with Andrea. Andrea was a girl from her class who also ignored her. Even though, she had tried to be friendly to Andrea, Andrea refused to talk. Andrea refused to even answer basic questions such as, "Did you have a good winter break?" Fortunately, the fact that Andrea ignored Sophie, allowed her to disappear without notice. She did so after carrying one box of orange juice upstairs.

Sophie made her way outside and found Zaragilda by the swing set. Together, they swung and swung and swung and swung. Up to the clouds. Higher and higher, they swung. Sophie was having so much fun, she didn't notice that her hat had fallen off her head. When she stopped swinging, Zaragilda looked at her.

"You're not one of us," Zaragilda said.

"Yes I am," Sophie insisted, reaching for her hat. It was then she realized that it was no longer on her head. She froze.

She looked towards her hat which was now lying on the ground. A yellow monster picked it up, "My hat, I found it!" Beaty stood next to him.

"See, I told you she was one of them," Beaty said.

Sophie's face went red and she ran off.

Chapter 6

Looking out the window from the classroom, Sophie watched the monsters play. Everyone in her class ignored her. She would never have someone to play tag with again. Nor would she have someone to climb a giant tower or to swing to the sky. This would be her life, with these classmates. Classmates who made her feel as if she was invisible.

Mrs. Cook assigned everyone a grammar worksheet. Standing beside Mrs. Cook was an assistant teacher. She helped Mrs. Cook by handing out the worksheets. While she was doing so, Mrs. Cook stepped out. Sophie started to fill out the worksheet. All of a sudden, it was ripped away from her. She looked up. Julia held it. She ripped it in half. Molly laughed.

"What are you going to do, Monster Girl?" Julia said. The other girls looked at their phones. Sophie felt a buzz. She looked at hers too. On it was a picture of her hanging out with Zaragilda.

Sophie ran toward the door of the classroom. She bumped into the assistant teacher. Flyers scattered everywhere. The assistant teacher bent down to pick them up. Sophie quickly slipped by her without notice.

Sophie ran through the hallways. Instead of running to the bathroom, she ran to the library. There, she had planned to hide behind one of the bookshelves. Yet, when she reached the library, she saw Mrs. Cook by the main desk. Sophie quickly turned around. The door? She could run out the door. Or ... she could go back to the classroom?

The thought of going back made her stomach turn. Outside however, the monsters could attack her. She was told they would. She was told they were vicious. However, when her hat fell off, they didn't attack her. Strange. Still, there was a risk. She took a breath and thought about what would make her happier.

With all her bravery, she opened the door.

Chapter 7

Sophie walked out the door and into the daylight. She took one step, then another and another. Suddenly, she was in the center of the monsters. Yet, nobody attacked her. Nobody called her any names. They ran around her, playing with one another. All different colors. They didn't even notice her. And ... she was fine.

"Hey," Zaragilda yelled.

Oh no. Sophie thought. This is it. Now, they would all look at me and attack me. Sophie sat down and made herself into a ball.

"Hey," Zaragilda yelled. "What are you doing?" Zaragilda laughed.

Sophie looked up.

Zaragilda's laughter wasn't mean or vicious. In fact, it sounded friendly.

Zaragilda held out her hand and pulled Sophie up.

"I thought you'd hate me," Sophie said.

"Hate you?" Zaragilda said, confused. "Why ever would I do that?"

"Well I don't know, because of the way I look, maybe?" Sophie answered, looking at her black and gray uniform and brown hair. Everyone here was a bright color and she was completely colorless.

"Sophie," Zaragilda said. "I told you that here, differences are good."

Sophie smiled.

"By the way, sorry about the hat yesterday. Beaty isn't the nicest. I got you this," Zaragilda held out a hat that was bright blue with gold stars. Sophie took it. She put it on.

Sophie smiled and ran off with her new friend towards the monkey bars. They swung and swung and swung. Sophie looked up toward her classroom. All her classmates looked out at her and for once, she didn't care.

9 780995 044166